The Popularity Papers

Love and Other Fiascos

With

Lydia Goldblatt

&

Julie Graham-Chang

Amulet Books
New York

Have you seen Roland today?

Nope, not yet.

When are you going to see him?

We have Math together, I'll probably see him then.

And then Julie + Roland = smoooooooooooooooooching.

Actually, I think we're working with graphs.

And then things will get graphic when you smoooch. Graphically.

I am ignoring you. A lot.

It has been two weeks since the party when a whole lot of people came over to see our band play and then Roland kind of sort of kissed me. During the last two weeks:

Jane and Chuck got back together.

I have seen Roland approximately 26 times.

Everyone thinks we're rock stars.

Two eighth-grade boys offered to help us make a music video to put on the Internet.

Then Jane and Chuck broke up again.

Don't you even care that some eighth graders want to make a video of me?

Am I supposed to?

You just don't GET ANYTHING.

Roland has not kissed me again. He hasn't kissed anyone else either, if that makes you feel any better.

Yay, Roland isn't an out-of-control kissing maniac.

I'm just trying to help.

Pucker up, World!!!

HOW JULIE SHOULD FEEL

Happy! Because Roland is a really great guy and would make a great boyfriend.

Tall, and can easily reach things

Multilingual, in case Julie ever needs to know how to say something in Norwegian

No longer has dippy haircut

Good kisser?

Confused! Because even though Roland is a really good friend, I can't tell if he wants to be my boyfriend or just stay friends.

ROLAND ASBJØRNSEN'S
ACTIONS

Over the Past Two Weeks

1. One time, when we were walking to class, he held my hand.

Verdict: Boyfriendy!

2. We hung out after school.

I was there.

Verdict: Friendy.

3. He passed me a note.

You look really nice today. Did you do the math homework?

The compliment seems Boyfriendy, but the math homework part seems not at all romantic.

Math isn't romantic?

No. No it is not.

Please try not to be mad, but I kind of sort of talked about the Roland Situation with a dating expert.

What? Who???

Jane.

WHY ARE YOU TALKING ABOUT MY BUSINESS TO JANE WHEN IT'S NONE OF HER BUSINESS AND NONE OF YOUR BUSINESS?

Okay, I feel like you didn't even try the whole not being mad thing.

I TRIED AND FAILED AND I'M OKAY WITH THAT. How is Jane an expert at dating?

She's dated Chuck a million times.

You waited to tell me this in note form so I couldn't strangle you in front of Mrs. Grubman.

Jane wants to talk to you. Just hear her out, okay?

HEAR YE, HEAR YE, gather round, for I have information of a personal nature to share with you. Listen close as I tell a tale that is absolutely none of my business! It is also none of your business! But listen up, because I am a huge blabber-mouth! It is an unfortunate incurable medical condition. So listen up!!!

Are you happy now that you've gotten that out of your system?

I don't think I made your mouth big enough.

Will you talk with Jane after school?

Do I have a choice? She's going to chase me down eventually.

We met with Jane after school and she had a lot of questions.

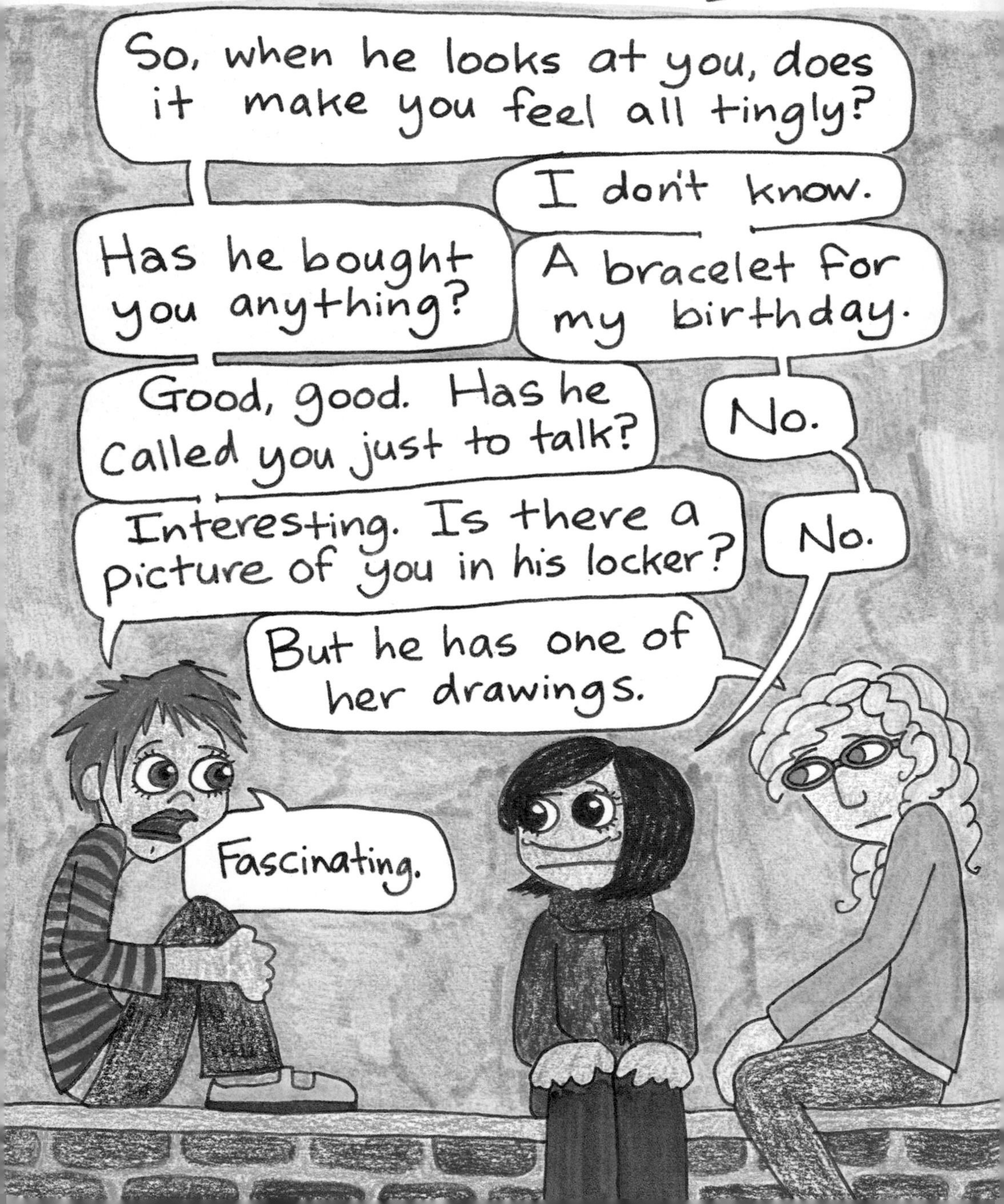

Then Jane said,

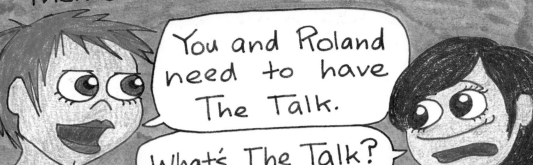

You and Roland need to have The Talk.

What's The Talk?

THE TALK

Apparently The Talk is a conversation that couples have when they want to figure out what's going on with their relationship. According to Jane, when things are confusing it's a woman's job to steer the man in the right direction.

Men are naturally confused about all of this and it's important to help them figure out what we want.

See? You would never have known any of this if I hadn't told Jane about your situation.

jladybugaboo: Do you think Jane's right about having The Talk?

goldstandard3000: Why not? Wouldn't it be better to make everything more clear?

jladybugaboo: What would your mom do?

goldstandard3000: Beats me, she doesn't talk about this stuff. Plus she's divorced, so I don't know how much she knows about romantic relationships. You should ask your dads, they've been together for a billion years.

jladybugaboo: I don't know. It's embarrassing.

goldstandard3000: But you've never been embarrassed to talk to them about anything.

jladybugaboo: I know. But they're men. What do they know about relationships with women?

goldstandard3000: I guess you can come over and ask my mom about it if you want to. Just remember that her track record with this sort of thing isn't that great.

jladybugaboo: Neither is Jane's…

goldstandard3000: You have a point.

Elaine Goldblatt, LUV GuRU

Yeah, right.

Talking to Mrs. Goldblatt was weird.

How can you tell if a guy likes you?

Well, he lets you know it.

How?

He communicates with you and misses you when you're gone and calls you and makes you feel like he can't live without you and sends you things and lets you know that he's thinking about you and plans to move across the ocean to be with you and accepts you for who you are.

That seems like a lot of work for Roland.

I told you she didn't know anything. You should just have The Talk.

Did you do it?
I did it!
Let me see the note!
Hei Roland, how are you?
I'm great! Are you great?
I'm okay. Hey, do you maybe want to hang out after school and have a talk?
Yes, I like talking with you. It is usually very pleasant.
Okay, great, so let's do that.
I am looking forward to it already!
So what do you think?
Does it sound like he can't live without me?
Seriously, don't listen to my mom. She's been super weird lately.

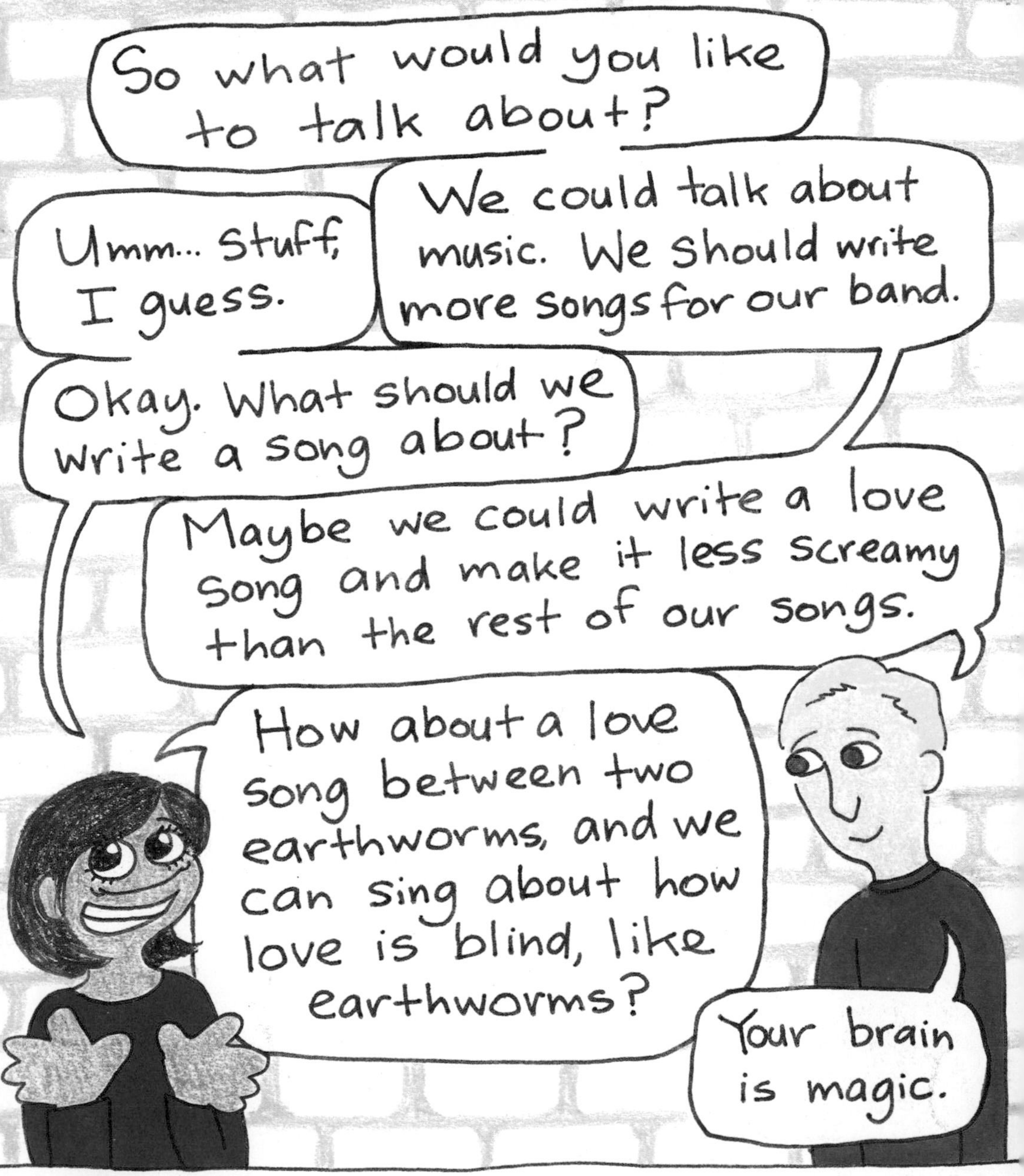

You might have dropped the ball.

Oh, you think???

goldstandard3000: ARE YOU THERE ARE YOU THERE ARE YOU THERE AREYOUTHERE???

jladybugaboo: Yes, All Caps, I'm here, and I don't feel like talking about my monumental communication failures.

goldstandard3000: Did you know that my mom is still dating Coach Eric???

jladybugaboo: Coach Eric from London? That Coach Eric?

goldstandard3000: No, the other Coach Eric.

jladybugaboo: There's another Coach Eric? She's dated two Coach Erics? That's weird. What does he coach?

goldstandard3000: WHY ISN'T THERE A SARCASM BUTTON ON THE INTERNET?

jladybugaboo: Sorry! Yet another communication failure. How is she dating him when he lives halfway around the world?

goldstandard3000: They never stopped talking to each other and got back together when she was working there last summer. She just told me.

jladybugaboo: So they don't really go on dates, though, because he's kind of a billion miles away.

goldstandard3000: Actually more like 3,526.

jladybugaboo: That's very specific.

goldstandard3000: I looked it up on the Internet. It's 6,909 miles to Abu Dhabi.

jladybugaboo: Good to know.

I feel like my mom would not have told me about the whole dating Coach Eric thing if it weren't important. When I talked to Melody I got the impression that she's known about it for a while.

It's great for Mom. Eric is a good guy.

How long have you known about this?

Don't we all just know things in our hearts sometimes?

I so wanted to go all ninja on her.

Violence is not the answer!!

I disagree!

Yesterday my mom made me say hi to Coach Eric when they were talking to each other on the computer.

It was strange. I felt like I was working really hard not to stare at my own face but I couldn't really help myself and then I was afraid I was making faces so I tried not to make faces, which made me make weirder faces.

Do you remember how hard it was for you to get the blue off of your hands after you dyed your hair?

Sure, why?

BECAUSE THAT'S HOW HARD IT IS TO GET JANE OFF MY BACK.

Did you have The Talk yet? You really need to have The Talk. The longer you go without having The Talk, the weirder it's going to be. If you don't have The Talk, then Roland can just start dating anyone else and you'll be b*t* I thought you were dating he can say, "But we never talked only action you'll be able to ke will be to cry and cry!!!

Now Jane is harassing me!

If you don't let Julie and Roland have some time alone, they're never going to have The Talk.

But the three of us always hang out after school.

No. You are hanging out with me after school today and we are going shopping.

But I don't need anything.

There's always something that you need! And right now you need to leave Julie and Roland ALONE.

Don't leave me!!!
I think I have to. Jane is TERRIFYING.

jladybugaboo: ARE YOU ONLINE???

goldstandard3000: Yes, how did it go?

jladybugaboo: I didn't have to do The Talk!

goldstandard3000: Really? Why not?

jladybugaboo: Because Roland beat me to it! He asked me out!!!

Do you like movies?

Yes. Movies are good.

Would you like to go to a movie with me?

That would be fun.

goldstandard3000: So Jane was right??? I was the one who was keeping him from asking you out?

jladybugaboo: I don't know. Let's not get all crazy and start thinking that Jane is right about stuff.

The Difference Between Going to the Movies and Going to the Movies ON A DATE

GOING to the MOVIES

And then...
So you're going to the movies alone with Roland because he asked you to go.
Well, yes, if that's okay with you.
Sure, honey, that's fine.
Wait a second, it's not fine just yet. So you want to be alone with Roland in a movie theater because he wants to be alone in a movie theater with you?
Umm, yes.
Is this a date? Did Roland ask you to go on a date with him?
I guess so.
You guess so or you know so?
I think so?

That's when Papa Dad left the room.

So is it okay if I go to the movies?

Which movie?

NO ONE IS SAYING YES TO ANYTHING JUST YET I AM WORKING ON SOMETHING.

Is Papa Dad Okay?

I'm not entirely certain.

I'M FINE NOBODY GO ANYWHERE I NEED A MINUTE STAY PUT.

Should we be worried?

Maybe a little.

While he was upstairs, Papa Dad wrote THIS.

Julie Graham-Chang's Rules for Dating
(to be applied from now until she is 30)

1. Julie is never to date anyone that has not first had a conversation lasting at least twenty minutes with at least one of her fathers.

2. If at least one of Julie's fathers does not like her date, then she is not allowed to date them. Ever.

3. Julie is to carry her cell phone and keep it on at all times during the course of her date, even if she's at the movie theater and is supposed to turn off her phone.

    a. If Julie's phone rings and it is one of her fathers calling she must pick up the phone, even if it's during the middle of a movie and she was supposed to turn her phone off.

4. Julie is never to be out alone with her date past 9 o'clock.

5. Julie and her date are never to be alone in a room with the door closed. The door must be open at all times.

6. Julie's fathers are allowed to make up more dating rules at any time.

Does Papa Dad want you to get in trouble with movie ushers? I really think he does.

Papa Dad is also insisting on having a mano-a-mano conversation with Roland before the date.

But Papa Dad talked to Roland a lot before the party. How much more talking do they need to do? They seemed pretty buddy-buddy.

That was before Roland asked me on an Official Date. Ever since he did that we've all been sucked into an alternate dimension where Roland is a dangerous criminal, Papa Dad has lost his mind, and Daddy is chill.

Even though Papa Dad is completely unhinged, I still get to go to the movies with Roland.

There's a showing of an old Norwegian movie, Flåklypa Grand Prix, at the Cinema Arts Center. Want to go?

Ja!

Julie, we need to TALK. xoxoxox Jane

What is that all about?

I should probably be a little scared, right?

Oh, most definitely.

JANE'S RULES for MOVIE DATES

No movies where you have to read anything on the screen. SUB-TITLES ARE WORK.

No comedies. Do you want to spend your whole date just sitting and laughing?

No documentaries. Dates are not the time to think.

So... when is the time to think?

NOW, dummy! Julie needs to do all her thinking now so she'll be prepared!

Horror movies are THE BEST. When something scary happens you can make your date feel like he's protecting you.

Why would I want to—

Let's practice! Okay, Julie, you be Roland, I'll be you, and Lydia, be scary.

AHHH!!! HOLD ME!

Boo?

Jane is TERRIFYING.
But is she wrong?

jladybugaboo: I asked Roland if he might want to see another movie.

goldstandard3000: And?

jladybugaboo: He seemed fine with it.

goldstandard3000: So what are you going to see?

jladybugaboo: Drill 4.

goldstandard3000: Isn't that the one with the dentist?

jladybugaboo: Don't tell me, I don't want to know.

goldstandard3000: Just close your eyes when you don't want to watch it. And let Roland protect you.

jladybugaboo: I guess. Hey, did you ever figure out how Jane knew what movie we were going to see in the first place?

goldstandard3000: I think she might be some sort of freaky clairvoyant.

TIME LEFT UNTIL DATE: 3 hours and 12 minutes

PREPARATIONS: Attire

TIME LEFT UNTIL DATE: 1 hour and 38 minutes
PREPARATIONS: Makeup

TIME LEFT UNTIL DATE: 27 minutes
PREPARATIONS: Papa Dad

You remember the rules.

Yes, Papa Dad.

I want you to have this.

What is it?

Pepper spray. If Roland tries anything funny, spray this into his eyes and run away screaming.

PAPA DAD.

Lydia, would you mind teaching Julie some last-minute self-defense moves if the pepper spray fails?

Walking away now...

DADDY! PAPA DAD IS FREAKING ME OUT!!!

Roland was right on time, and then the interrogation began.

Hello Roland.

Hi Mr. Graham, how are you?

Wouldn't you like to know.

I would, thank you!

Oh... I'm okay.

I'm glad!

I think Papa Dad was trying to make Roland scared of him, but
  a. Papa Dad isn't scary
  b. Roland isn't so great at taking hints
After a while Julé dragged Roland out of the house and Mrs. Asbjørnsen drove them to the movies.

Jane and I walked back to my house to wait for her mom to pick her up.

Looks like it's just you and me now. Us single girls have to stick together.

What do you mean?

Julie's with Roland now. She's got better things to do than hang out with us all the time.

She can hang out with us and Roland at the same time, just like we always do.

Oh Lydia, Lydia, Lydia.

What what what?

Things are about to get seriously different.

After Mrs. Astley picked Jane up my mom declared a "Goldblatt Girl" meeting.

Girls... I have to confess something. I've been keeping a secret from you. This past summer when I was working in London...

ERIC ASKED ME TO MARRY HIM!

WHAT?

Are you making us move back to England?

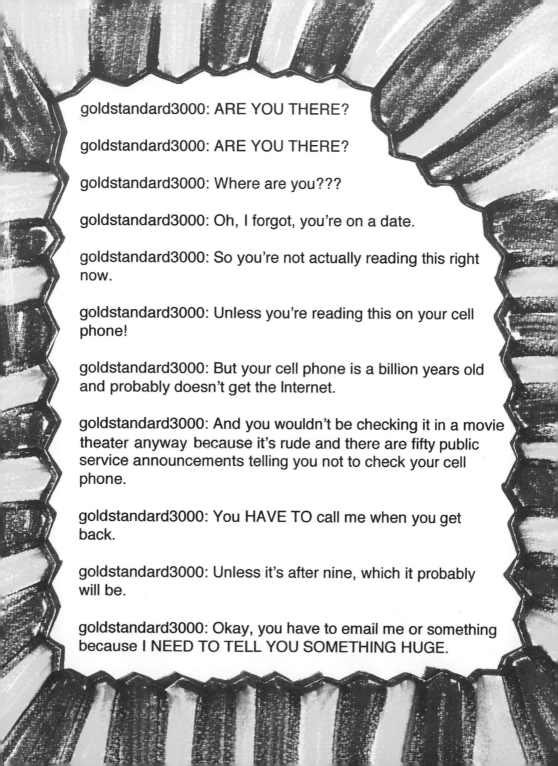

goldstandard3000: ARE YOU THERE?

goldstandard3000: ARE YOU THERE?

goldstandard3000: Where are you???

goldstandard3000: Oh, I forgot, you're on a date.

goldstandard3000: So you're not actually reading this right now.

goldstandard3000: Unless you're reading this on your cell phone!

goldstandard3000: But your cell phone is a billion years old and probably doesn't get the Internet.

goldstandard3000: And you wouldn't be checking it in a movie theater anyway because it's rude and there are fifty public service announcements telling you not to check your cell phone.

goldstandard3000: You HAVE TO call me when you get back.

goldstandard3000: Unless it's after nine, which it probably will be.

goldstandard3000: Okay, you have to email me or something because I NEED TO TELL YOU SOMETHING HUGE.

What It's Like to Try to Sleep When You Have HUGE NEWS and You Can't Get in Touch with Your Best Friend

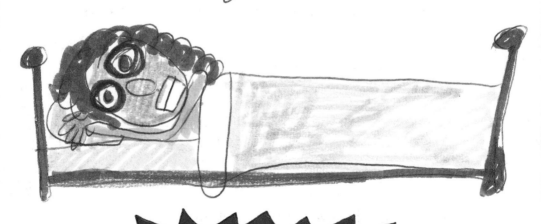

jladybugaboo: What?

jladybugaboo: What?

jladybugaboo: What???

I tried to find Lydia before homeroom, but Jane found me first.

Oh my god, Julie, tell me EVERYTHING RIGHT NOW!!!

I kind of didn't know what to tell her.

I had a nice time.

This was sort of true.

GIVE ME DETAILS, WOMAN!!!

Thank goodness for homeroom bells.

Hey, lookit the time, gotta go!!!

The Details

It was kind of strange to be alone with Roland, even though we've been alone together a million times. Oh, and his mom was there.

So I am going to pick you up after the movie is over, okay? Like a fancy limousine driver. The limousine is fancy, not me, the driver. English can be very confusing.

Mor...*

Ignore me! It is like I am not even here. The car is driving itself!

* Norwegian for "mother"

Then it was bad, but still okay.

Then it was not okay at all.

I started to wonder if Roland expected us to be kissing, too, but I didn't want to kiss, because I felt like that's what the movie wanted me to do, so I just stared straight ahead without blinking. It was extra awkward.

What did you need to tell me?

Later, I don't want to put it all in a note.

Tell me.

Later.

Tell me.

Later.

TELL ME TELL ME TELL ME!!!!

Later Later Later!!!!! Jeez, you're annoying.

Hmmm... wonder who I picked that up from...

I finally got a chance to talk with Julie at lunch, but then...

So last night my mom called a meeting...

Gah! Lydia! Nobody cares. Did Roland kiss you?

There wasn't really a good time.

What do you mean there wasn't a good time??? How is that possible? You were at Drill 4!

I didn't know it was a romance.

Let's talk after school.

jladybugaboo: Where did you go after school?

goldstandard3000: I guess we just wanted to give you and Roland a chance to be together alone.

jladybugaboo: Oh. Thanks. So what's going on? Might as well just tell me.

The GOLDBLATT SITUATION

Over the summer, while we were in a car with Daddy and Papa Dad

and Melody was off in Guatemala getting bald and weird

Mrs. Goldblatt and Coach Eric were on the Smooch Train to Engagementville.

Mrs. Goldblatt kept the engagement a secret while they were working out the details — because Coach Eric is coming to live in the United States, they have to go through all sorts of immigration stuff, which takes time (like when I was adopted).

13 YEARS AGO

They're telling me that we'll probably be able to come home in about two weeks. Is the nursery ready?

Don't worry, it's been ready for ages. How's our sweet baby?

So great. She barfed on me twice today.

Give her ten thousand kisses for me and tell her I'll see her soon.

Now that the immigration stuff has been sorted out, Coach Eric is coming to live with the Goldblatts and then he and Mrs. Goldblatt are going to get married.

Mr. and Mrs.
Coach Eric
Iforgothislastname
Wexler

jladybugaboo: Wow. Are you okay with that?

goldstandard3000: I guess so. Things are about to get seriously different.

jladybugaboo: How about Melody? What does she think?

goldstandard3000: She's so weird.

jladybugaboo: How?

goldstandard3000: She's just been super quiet about it.

It looks like romance is in the air...

Oh right, Roland. Sorry I haven't asked you about that, I've been a little distracted.

No no no, Jane.

Oh no. Seriously?

Yep.

Again?!?

AGAIN.

Jules! Guess who's back in the couples club?

Uh...

It's me! And Chuck. We're back together!

Great?

Want to come over after school? My mom is making me look through forty thousand bridal magazines. We have to stop her from getting something too poofy.

Or something...

EXTRA POOFY!!!

It's eating her alive!!!

Nuts, I forgot, Jane's making me and Roland hang out with her and Chuck after school.

What are you going to do?

I think we're just going to Chuck's house. Wanna come?

I think I'll pass.

I have discovered that bridal magazines are all one hundred pages of booooooooooring.

What do you think about this one?

It's white.

And this one?

Also white?

Thank you for your input. Where's Melody?

Maybe I should have gone with Julie to her Couples Club.

What It's Like to Hang Out with Jane and Chuck.

I don't think I'll ever get that slurping sound out of my head. Looking through forty thousand bridal magazines sounds like a good time right now.

jladybugaboo: How'd the wedding planning go?

goldstandard3000: After looking through a pile of them my mom said that we just have to go to bridal shops to see which styles look good on her.

jladybugaboo: Bridal shopS? Like, more than one?

goldstandard3000: More than one. AND YOU ARE GOING WITH US.

jladybugaboo: Oh, I think I have something to do that day.

goldstandard3000: I never said what day it was. YOU ARE GOING WITH US.

jladybugaboo: Is Melody going as well?

goldstandard3000: I don't know. She managed to avoid the magazines by staying in her room the entire time.

jladybugaboo: Such a simple yet effective plan.

goldstandard3000: Wish I had thought of it. So did you have fun at Chuck's?

jladybugaboo: Depends on your interpretation of fun.

goldstandard3000: ?

jladybugaboo: Let's just say that while some people might think two hours of watching Jane and Chuck face wrestle is fun, I am not one of those people.

Dress Shopping Day!

Today is going to be SO MUCH FUN!!!

Where's Melody for the fun?
She said that she had "a thing."
"A thing"? That's some lazy excuse- making.
I know, right?

Our first stop →

Lady McFancyface's Bridal Boutique

The woman at the first bridal shop could not have had a bigger smile.

We are going to find your dress, Elaine. The Dress. The Dress that was MEANT FOR YOU.

Except when she saw my hair.

And are you going to be in the wedding?

They both are!

I am?

You totally cried.
There was something in my eye.
You're pretty much my family, you know.

Sometimes people ask me who my real mother is. It's pretty annoying because if I had a mom and a dad instead of two dads, probably no one would ask me that.

I have two parents, so I'm lucky.

But seriously, don't you want to know who your real mom is?

The truth is that my birth mother couldn't take care of a kid, and my dads really, really wanted to, so they're my real parents. And Lydia's mom wants me, too, so anyone who can't see how lucky I am is clueless.

Mom's looking at shiny pink bridesmaid dresses.

Then again, maybe I'm not THAT lucky.

We managed to pull the bride away from the shiny pinkness to focus on her own dress.

Big Smile was getting annoyed with us, so we left to get lunch. That's when we came up with

THE BEST PLAN EVER

We didn't even have to discuss it. It just sort of happened.

So what color are we thinking for your dresses?

Dark red!

Aqua!

Or we could each have our own color...

And Melody can wear pink!

And that's what she gets for bailing on us today.
It was a beautiful moment.

After lunch we went to another bridal shop.

DRESS O' RAMA

And then we went into a coma.

Ladies, what do we think?

Beautiful. It's The One.

Love it.

I do, too. I figured that taking us to the salon was my mom's way of saying, "Please don't have blue hair in my wedding album." Plus I've been kind of tired of the color ever since Jane dyed her hair blue, too.

Papa Dad is going to miss his Smurf jokes.   He is the only one.

When our big Lady Day was finally over, I came home to find an inbox full of Jane's emails.

princessj8: OMG where are you we're going to Chuck's if you don't come Roland will be all alone write back

princessj8: Where are you seriously annoyed

princessj8: Fine going without you but you have to write back

And one from Roland.

blomkal1: How did the shopping go? Did Lydia's mom find a dress that she liked?

I don't get why Jane's freaking out. I had legitimate other plans.

Can I staple this tracking device to your head? Thanx!

I was all excited to tell Mel about the fantastic new ultra-pink dress that she'd be wearing for the wedding, but she was in a weird place.

You will not believe the super-awesome dress we found for you...

Stop. We need to talk.

About your fantastic dress? Because it's pink. Really extra pink.

I won't be wearing a bridesmaid dress, and neither will you.

And then Melody told me something that freaked me out.

Did Mom tell you that Eric has kids?

Sure. Why?

He has a boy and a girl. And if he comes here to live with us he'll be leaving them behind in England.

See yas!

Just like Dad left us when he married Brenna and moved to Colorado.

goldstandard3000: So Melody wants us to sabotage the wedding.

jladybugaboo: Really? Oh my god.

goldstandard3000: Well, not really. She just wants us to find a way to let Mom know that we don't approve of Coach Eric.

jladybugaboo: But you do approve of Coach Eric.

goldstandard3000: I did, but that was before I knew that he was going to abandon his kids.

jladybugaboo: It's weird that your mom would even let him do that for her.

goldstandard3000: You saw her at the bridal shop. She's under some sort of Crazy Lady Love Spell. If love makes a person act this selfish, I never want to be in a relationship.

jladybugaboo: I don't think that all relationships make you all Crazy Lady.

goldstandard3000: How many emails did you get from Jane?

jladybugaboo: Point taken. So what are you going to do?

goldstandard3000: I don't know.

Love hasn't made me crazy. Whatever would make you think that?

Thoughts on
BEING in a RELATIONSHIP

I don't think that dating Roland has made me crazy, but how would I know? The thing about crazy people is that they never think that they're crazy.

> Love hasn't made me crazy. Whatever would make you think that?

But I don't think that I'm the same person that I was before Roland and I started dating. At least people don't seem to see me the same way.

Now that I'm in a relationship, I feel like I have to do things that I really don't like doing.

1. Hanging out with random other couples just because we're all couples.

2. Talking about other people who might or might not be part of a couple.

Also, ever since we started dating, Roland and I can't seem to hang out alone. We're always surrounded by other people (even when we're not with other couples).

Who's ready to watch a documentary about a font?

I don't even know if I really want to hang out alone with Roland, but I'd like to at least give it a try.

So do you have any ideas about how we're going to break up my mom and Eric?

No, I haven't had a moment to think. Did you know that Ross and Deirdre might be a thing?

A thing? Like what sort of thing?

I have no idea. What's Mel's plan to break them up?

Sit around being mopey and not talking to anyone.

That's a stupid plan.

She's terrible at this.

Let's hang out this afternoon and figure something out.

Don't you have to hang out with Roland?

No, I can hang out with you today.

Okay.

When I asked Melody what our plan was to make sure that Coach Eric didn't abandon his kids for us, she was extremely unhelpful.

We just have to make it clear to Mom that her impending nuptials are damaging us.

And how do we do that?

By being damaged in front of her, duh.

Melody really is the worst at this.

I know!!!

The only thing worse than Melody's "plan" is her follow-through.

After all this time of keeping a research journal of the behaviors of others, certainly we can come up with a better plan.

At the very least, we can't come up with a _worse_ plan. Yay us!

OPERATION SABOTAGE

Our plan, should we choose to accept it (which, duh, we do):

Make the house as unwelcoming as possible. We have to find out what sort of things Men don't like, and then we're going to make sure that the house is full of those things so that Eric can't get comfortable.

Things that
MEN DON'T LIKE

I think we need to find some men
and ask them what they don't like.

WHAT MEN DON'T LIKE

Stinky perfumes.

Women should smell strongly of fish.

I think Roland's older brothers are messing with me.

They might be right—Daddy also mentioned that he didn't like strong perfumes.

Yeah, but Pete and Anders offered me stinky fish paste.

Just dab some behind your ears, Roland will love it!

jladybugaboo: Well, what did Mel say?

goldstandard3000: She actually likes the plan!

jladybugaboo: Really???

goldstandard3000: Yes! She said that asserting our feminine dominance was a great idea, and that her friend Declan can drive us to Frillows this weekend to pick up some stuff for the house.

jladybugaboo: Awesome! Let's assert our feminine dominance all over that store!

goldstandard3000: Wait, don't you have to hang out with Roland this weekend?

jladybugaboo: Don't worry, I can get out of it.

goldstandard3000: Are you sure?

jladybugaboo: I need to assert my feminine dominance on some throw pillows.

goldstandard3000: Yay!

It's not that I don't like hanging out with Roland, but maybe I actually don't like hanging out with Roland. I used to, but now things are all weird.

It's like we're friends but then he'll go and hold my hand and I get all weirded out, because I feel like my hand is sweaty, and I don't want to hurt his feelings by letting go of his hand, but then I don't know when to let go of his hand...it's all very complicated.

Handholding: A Guide to Letting Go

1. He grabs your hand.

2. You start to want your hand back.

a.) You yank it out of his hand, causing him sadness.

But why?

b.) You leave your hand where it is, and spend the rest of your life attached to him while being able to use only one hand.

c.) You say you have to go to the bathroom.

Roland must think I have a bladder-control problem. Going to Frillows is so much easier than figuring all this out.

Somehow Melody convinced Elaine to give us money to spend on

Things to make the house more welcoming for Eric!

Melody's friend Declan drove us to Frillows. It was weird to be riding in a car that was being driven by someone only a few years older than us.

Can you believe that Melody is almost old enough to drive?

Weird. Hey, do you think that she and Declan are a thing?

What sort of thing?

You, know, like a couple.

Melody?? Gross. Now my brain hurts.

And then we were at Frillows.

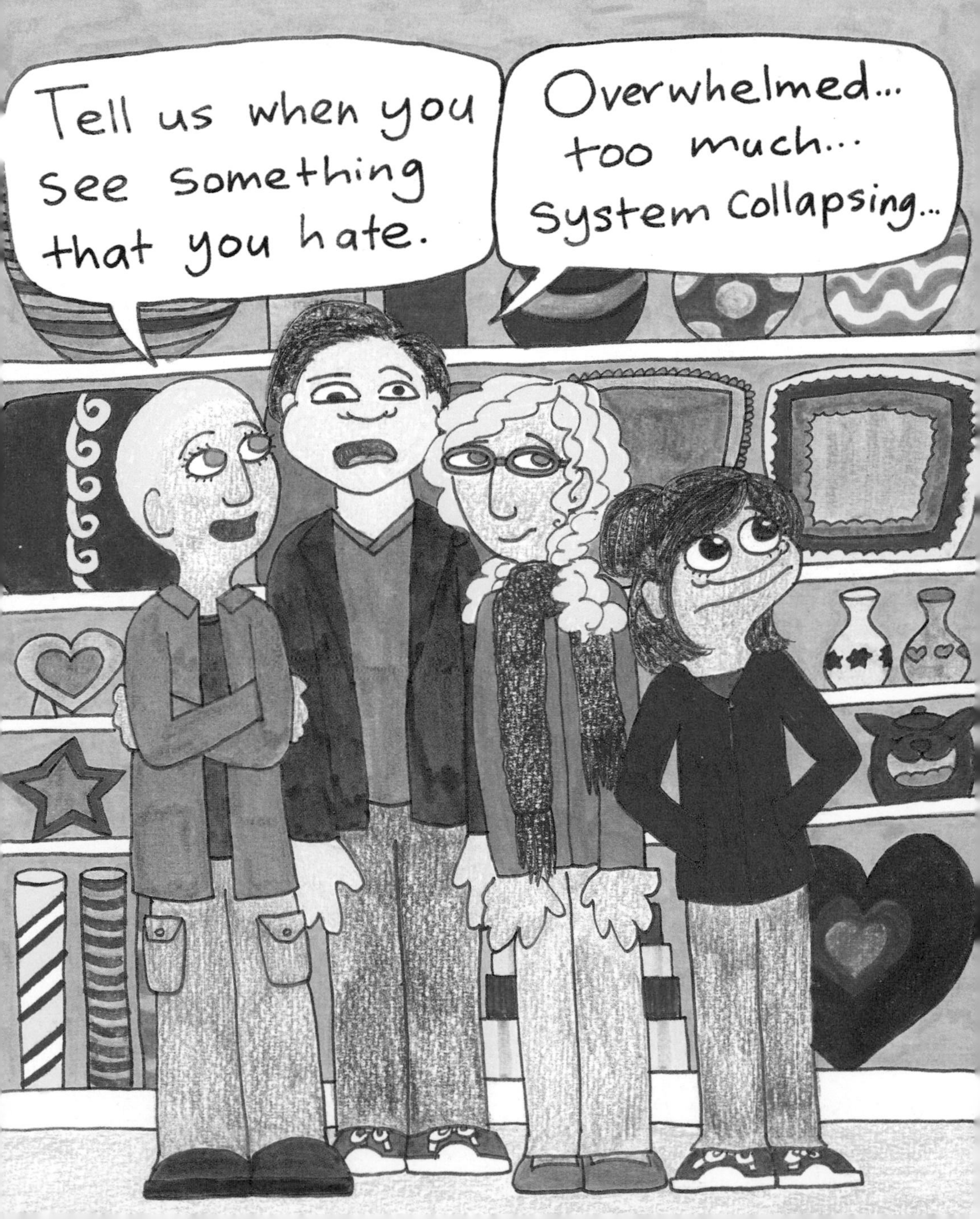

OBJECTS of his DISAFFECTION

CANDLES

This one smells like a vanilla bean stabbing a pumpkin pie.

POTPOURRI

It's like beef jerky for flowers!

DECORATIVE PILLOWS

Why, WHY would you sew glass beads to a pillow? How could that possibly be comfortable?

Poor pillow. You deserved better.

Eventually Declan couldn't take it anymore and we had to go. We thought we'd done pretty well, but Melody felt like we could do more.

When we got home Mom was so pleased that we'd gone out of our way to make the house more welcoming for Coach Eric, and for a moment I felt terrible that we were working to ruin her happiness.

It was hard to keep Coach Eric's poor abandoned kids in mind.

goldstandard3000: Do you really think that we're doing the right thing? I mean, it's not like Coach Eric's kids back in England will actually be porridgeless and starving.

jladybugaboo: Probably not.

goldstandard3000: Probably not, his kids won't starve, or we're probably not doing the right thing?

jladybugaboo: I don't think they're going to starve. I also have doubts that porridgeless is a word.

goldstandard3000: But we're doing the right thing?

jladybugaboo: I think so. I mean, I know your mom seems happy right now but some people probably just shouldn't be together.

goldstandard3000: Who are you thinking about?

jladybugaboo: I don't know. Some couples we know.

goldstandard3000: Jane and Chuck? But they seem perfect for each other!

jladybugaboo: ????

goldstandard3000: HA HA HA just kidding.

jladybugaboo: Don't joke, I have to hang out with them tomorrow…

TYPICAL TIMELINE OF JANE & CHUCK'S RELATIONSHIP

1. After being broken up for a while, Jane and Chuck get back together.

We're back together!

But **WHY**!??

It is a mystery.

2. Jane and Chuck schmoop all over each other, causing everyone in a five-mile radius to spontaneously vomit.

It's a public health problem.

4. And last (but not least!)
BIG PUBLIC FIGHTS!

I HATE YOU!

OF COURSE YOU DO!

SHUT UP, CHUCK!

So are you hanging out with them this afternoon?
Probably.

I need to find something to do after school now that all of my bandmates are dating each other. It's sort of lame that I can't hang out with Julie and Roland anymore, but I don't want to be a third wheel. I also don't want to go immediately home after school because Melody keeps cornering me.

We need to work on stopping the wedding.

She's **OBSESSED**. And still awful at plotting.

Let's disconnect the Internet so Mom can't talk to Eric!

But then we won't have the Internet. You're terrible at this.

And when I'm not listening to Melody coming up with dumb plans, I have to listen to my mom coming up with wedding plans for the wedding we're trying to stop.

So what do you think? I like calla lilies but Eric likes roses but he says it's my choice...

Umm...

Oh, I don't know, gerbera daisies are nice. So are tulips... Help!!!

Roland and I are going to hang out with Jane and Chuck at Chuck's place after school. Want to come?

And watch a big make-out party? Oh goody!

Roland and I don't make out. We can all play cards or something.

Nah, I've got other plans.

Really? Who with?

Jen and I are doing something.

What?

I don't know. Jen stuff?

JEN STUFF:

Let's learn how to read Ancient Greek.

Hanging out with Jen is always an experience.

Us single girls have to stick together.

Literally? Do you have a plan for going to the bathroom?

I like Jen, she's my friend, but sometimes I can't tell when she's kidding or really being serious.

Maybe we can do something with Velcro so that we can detach when one of us needs to pee.

But hanging out with Jen is still more fun than going home to deal with wedding and anti-wedding craziness.

Let's knit a wrap for this tree.

Why?

I saw some on a few trees when my mom took me to Philadelphia.

Can you even knit?

No, but you could teach me.

Super weird. But okay.

So now we're knitting for trees. Still better than going home.

jladybugaboo: Guess which couple just hit Stage 3?
goldstandard3000: In front of you and Roland?
jladybugaboo: Oh yes.
What do you mean you can't come over for dinner tomorrow?
I have a thing.
A THING? What kind of THING?
I made plans ages ago, and you just told me about dinner five seconds ago.
PLANS? Plans for things? Why won't you tell me about your THING PLANS?

goldstandard3000: What did you do?
jladybugaboo: The only thing we could do.
goldstandard3000: You hid in the bathroom?
jladybugaboo: We totally hid in the bathroom.
Are you Crying?
I may be having an allergic reaction to these Soaps.
Should we go back to the den?
WHY ARE YOU SO AFRAID TO OPEN UP TO MEEEEE?
I think I'd rather sneeze to death.

goldstandard3000: You guys really need to start hanging out without Jane and Chuck. It's just going to get worse.

jladybugaboo: You're right. Maybe we can hang out with you and Jen? Wrapping trees in yarn sounds cool.

goldstandard3000: It does?

jladybugaboo: Maybe?

goldstandard3000: No, you guys should go on a real date. Just have fun with each other and stuff.

jladybugaboo: I guess so. Roland keeps suggesting ice-skating.

goldstandard3000: That sounds fun! You should go.

jladybugaboo: But I don't know how to skate. I'll break every bone in my body. It might be safer to keep hanging out with Jane and Chuck.

goldstandard3000: You have to go! Roland will help you. It will be romantic.

jladybugaboo: Falling on my butt is romantic?

goldstandard3000: More romantic than hiding in a bathroom or standing out in the freezing cold making a sweater for a tree.

Did you pretend to go upstairs and then listen in?
We can't trust that boy.
You have to calm down. Roland is a sweetie.
A Sweetie? Are you forgetting that he's from Viking stock? And that Viking maidens were usually married by the time they were 13? Julie is 13!!!
Okay, we're switching you to decaf.

Papa Dad has totally lost his mind.
I'm not surprised. Papa Dad
has always been overprotective of you.
What do you mean?
Umm... The Hair-Pulling Incident?

If your son pulls my daughter's hair one more time

I'm taping his fingers together.

In the end Daddy convinced Papa Dad to let me go skating with Roland, although he made me promise to wear my skateboarding safety gear.

Romantic!

What It's Like to Learn to Skate

I am ouch all over. But it was kind of fun. And I thought that Roland was going to kiss me again, BUT...

AWKWARD.

goldstandard3000: How did it go?

jladybugaboo: You were right—it was a lot more fun than watching Jane and Chuck be Jane and Chuck.

goldstandard3000: Intensive dentistry is more fun than watching Jane and Chuck be Jane and Chuck.

jladybugaboo: True. But then Papa Dad was watching us the whole time, so that wasn't so fun.

goldstandard3000: You need to have a talk with him.

jladybugaboo: Yeah, I don't see that working out.

Tomorrow is Eric's Move-In Day.

And after your flight lands we'll head straight home!

I can't wait to see you.

All of the preparations have been made, but Melody still doesn't think it's enough.

We'll have to wait until he gets here and then figure out what the next step is.

That's not scary at all.

jladybugaboo: Is he there? How does he like the beaded throw pillows?

goldstandard3000: So far he totally hasn't noticed. He's just all googly-eyed for my mom.

jladybugaboo: That's kind of sweet. ?

goldstandard3000: It's actually super sweet.

Schmoooooooop!!

goldstandard3000: I've never seen my mom so happy.

jladybugaboo: So are you still going ahead with the sabotage?

goldstandard3000: I don't know. But Melody wants to.

So what is Melody doing?

Nothing so far, besides hiding out in her room.

Maybe she's given up.

I don't think so. She seemed pretty determined the other day.

What are you going to do?

Avoid home. Jen and I are going to wrap a tree after school.

Where? Maybe Roland and I can help.

Don't worry about it, it's really just a two-person job.

Wrapping trees is kind of fun. Jen picked up knitting really quickly — she's smart like that. She also has a knack for picking good trees.

I like hanging out with Jen but sometimes I wish we could spend more time with Julie and Roland, like we used to.

Being friends with a couple is lame because they need Couple Time, and the only other people who can be with them are Couples.

So get a boyfriend.

It's not that easy.

Sure it is!

I honestly don't know how I could have handled that better.

I think I have food poisoning, gotta go, bye!

And then I had to listen to Jamie Burke tell me about the time he had food poisoning.

What's interesting is that I had just eaten sushi, and you can really see the seaweed when it comes back up.

Oh.

I couldn't believe that Jen told Jamie Burke that I wanted a boyfriend. He is obviously not boyfriend material.

WAYS THAT JAMIE BURKE IS NOT BOYFRIEND MATERIAL

1. In second grade Jamie asked every girl in our class to marry him, so he can't be taken seriously.

Everyone at school knows that Jamie asked Lydia out. If they didn't see his first proposal, they probably saw his second one.
Want to go out with me?
GAH!
Or the third one.
So how about we go on a date?
GAH!
Where did you even come from?

People are really starting to talk about the whole Jamie Burke Situation.

Dr. Embarrassed.

Is the coast clear?

I think so.

You thought so last time.

He's way faster and sneakier than you'd think.

Okay, so here's the plan — you leave class first, and I'll hide behind you, and if he shows up you talk to him while I make a run for it.

Maybe you should just tell him that you're not interested.

Isn't making a run for it sort of the same thing as telling him I'm not interested?

Just in case you haven't noticed, Jamie's not the best at taking hints.

I just don't want to deal with it. Mom's wedding is coming up and I've got bigger things to deal with.

What's it like to live with Eric?

What It's Like to Have Coach Eric Living with Us

1. My mom is super happy all the time.

2. Melody spends all her time in her room.

3. There are way too many stupid pillows.

④ Our house has become wedding preparation central.

5.) Coach Eric has no idea how to load the dishwasher.

He doesn't separate the silverware.

 Right Way

 Coach Eric's Way

small forks	big forks	sharp knives
small spoons	big spoons	butter knives

any old utensil	random forks and knives	plastic straws? ???
maybe one spoon	empty for no reason	what-ever

The horror!

There's no need to be sarcastic.

I wasn't being sarcastic. That is definitely the wrong way to load a dishwasher. It's like he's asking to be stabbed by a misplaced knife.

That's what I said, thank you! When we're older we should totally live together.

135

Mom and Eric have decided to have their wedding on New Year's Eve, because it's easier for his kids to come when they're not in school. He's getting excited about them coming over, and the more excited he gets, the more angry Melody becomes.

Oh, I'm sure you're just thrilled to have them here for a few days before you ship them back to England.

I know. I wish they'd come to live here, but Ellie has only one year left at university and there's no tearing David away from his girlfriend.

Coach Eric's kids are **OLD.**
Like, how old?
David graduated from college
TWO YEARS AGO. They're in
their twenties! They're crazy old.
That's great! So it's not like Coach
Eric is really an abandoner and
now Melody can relax.
You'd think so, right? But no.

I wouldn't believe
it, but I kind of
miss Hippy Dippy
Let's Share Our
Feelings Melody.

137

goldstandard3000: New problem.

jladybugaboo: Yay! What now?

goldstandard3000: My mom found out that you and Roland are dating and thinks it's SO CUTE.

jladybugaboo: Barf.

goldstandard3000: She wants him to come to the wedding as your date.

jladybugaboo: What? Why? Does she want to watch Papa Dad stare angrily at him all night?

goldstandard3000: Wait, it gets worse. Mom told Melody and me that we could bring our own dates, too.

jladybugaboo: Who are you going to bring?

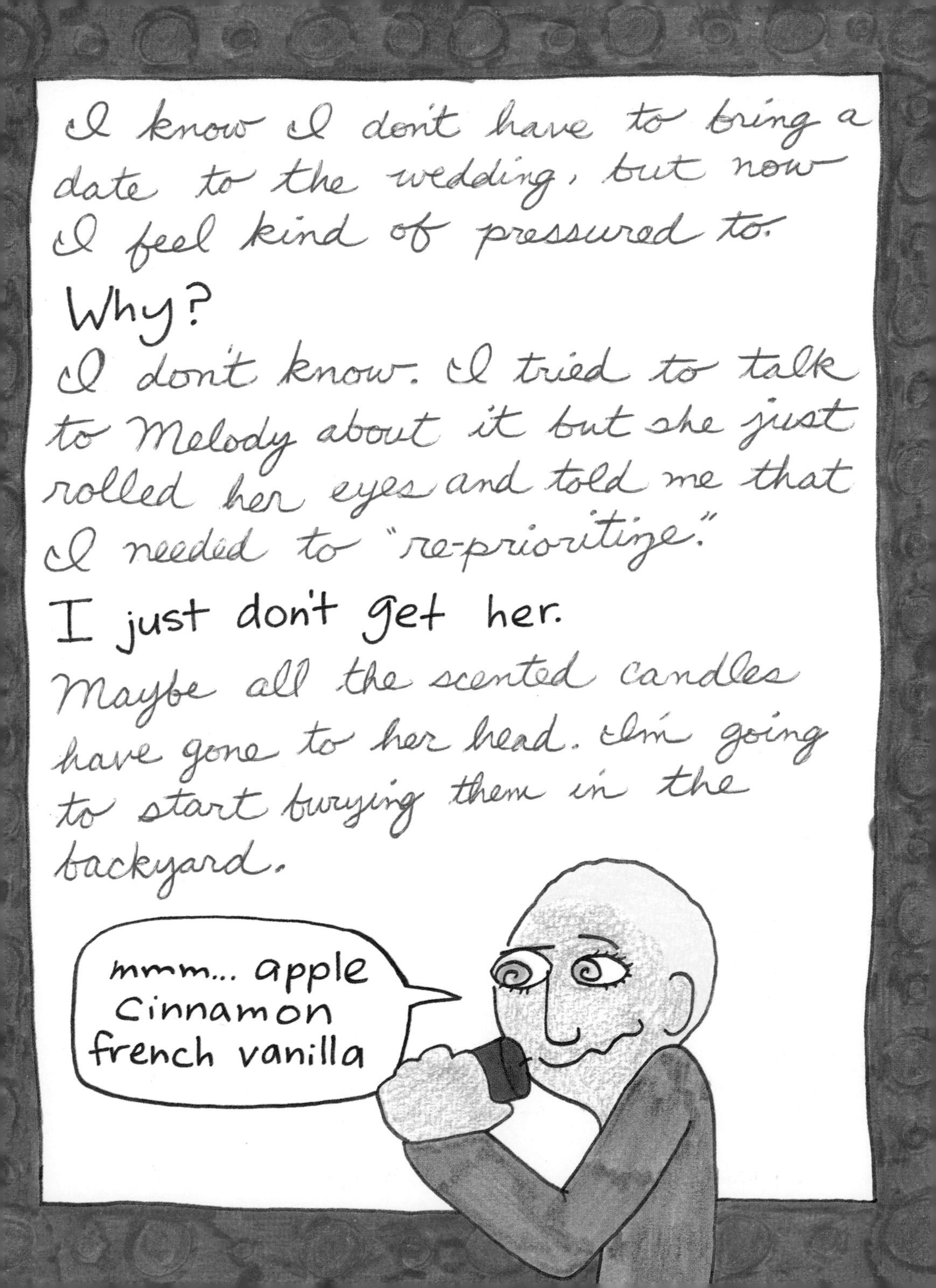
I know I don't have to bring a date to the wedding, but now I feel kind of pressured to.
Why?
I don't know. I tried to talk to Melody about it but she just rolled her eyes and told me that I needed to "re-prioritize."
I just don't get her.
Maybe all the scented candles have gone to her head. I'm going to start burying them in the backyard.
mmm... apple cinnamon french vanilla

I can't believe he did this.

Will you go out with me Lydia Goldblatt?

Maybe you should go out with him.
It's not every day someone gets
in-school suspension for you.

Oh good god. I'm going to go on
a date with Jamie Burke.

So where are you going to go
On your big date?

I don't know. The moment I told Jamie that I'd go on one date with him, he ran down the hallway screaming "SHE SAID YES!!!"

Yeesh. Roland wants me to spend Christmas Eve with his family.

That's nice. Are you going to go?

Maybe. They have some weird traditions. Roland says that in Norway a goat-elf named Julebukk gives you presents and that we're all supposed to dress like goats and go door-to-door asking for candy.

A goat-elf?

Also, if we don't leave a bowl of porridge out for a gnome named Nisse, he will play tricks on us and stop guarding our farm animals.

Do you ever wonder if Roland makes this stuff up to mess with us?

So I asked Papa Dad if I could spend Christmas Eve with the Asbjørnsens. It did not go well.

Christmas Eve? But we have traditions.

What traditions?

Getting Chinese food with the Goldblatts is a sort of tradition.

I don't know what to do. He didn't exactly say no, but he also hasn't been making a lot of sense since Roland first asked me out.

goldstandard3000: Are you there? Are you online?

jladybugaboo: Yes, what?

goldstandard3000: We just had a video chat with Coach Eric's kids.

jladybugaboo: How did it go?

I thought it was going well, but after less than a minute Melody excused herself. A little while later I went to see what happened to her and she was crying.

I thought that went well— why are you crying?

Why couldn't our dad have waited until we were in college to move thousands of miles away?

I didn't know what to tell her— I'd never seen Melody cry before, not even that time when she burned her hand on the stove. Maybe she'll feel better when the wedding is over.

Coach Eric's kids and Lori are coming to stay with us and then going to New York for a few days to do some sightseeing before the wedding. Mom is getting a little frantic with all the preparations.

My **TO DO** List

> ## Lydia's To Do List
>
> 1. Please learn how to play "In My Life" on your guitar so that Eric and I can dance to you playing our favorite song.

That's a short list.

I am going to have to spend every single waking minute practicing until the wedding.

What about your date with Jamie?

Maybe next year?

We need to have a talk.

Why? What's up?

Your boyfriend is a Meddler.

Meddler: med·dler

1. One who meddles; one who interferes or busies himself with things in which he has no concern; a busybody

2. Roland Asbjørnsen, who just invited Jamie Burke to spend Christmas Eve with Lydia at his house

We're going to have a great time, my little sugar plum!

Oh dear god.

When I talked to Roland about inviting Jamie and Lydia over for Christmas Eve at his house, he didn't seem to think he'd done anything wrong.

But I thought it would be fun. The more, the more merry, yes?

But Lydia has a lot to do before the wedding and she's stressed out.

Jamie will distract her. It's perfect!

Aaargh!

I'll just practice my guitar the entire time. Everyone will just have to understand. Yay?

All of a sudden it feels like everything is being planned for me.

And no one seems to care what I want to do.
Join the club.

goldstandard3000: EMERGENCY.

jladybugaboo: Your dress doesn't fit? I'm wearing mine right now.

goldstandard3000: MELODY IS GONE.

jladybugaboo: What do you mean? We're meeting for tea in less than an hour.

goldstandard3000: SHE'S GONE.

jladybugaboo: Are you sure she's not just in the bathroom or something and you're just freaking out because you've been under a little bit of stress?

goldstandard3000: SHE LEFT A MESSAGE.

STICKY NOTE

OF DOOM

TELL MOM NOT TO WORRY, I JUST HAVE TO TAKE CARE OF SOME UNFINISHED BUSINESS AND I'LL BE BACK IN TIME FOR NEW YEAR'S.
—M

jladybugaboo: What does that mean?!?

goldstandard3000: It means that my mother is going to kill me.

jladybugaboo: But you didn't do anything!

goldstandard3000: But I'm here and available for the killing!!!

jladybugaboo: Where could she have gone?

Places Where Melody Could Have Gone to Take Care of "Unfinished Business"

1. Guatemala: Maybe she didn't finish something there last summer?

   That's a pretty long trip.

2. Gretchen's house: Maybe she's still upset with Gretchen's sister for being mean to her in sixth grade?

   That seems pretty unlikely.

3. The yarn shop: Maybe she ran out of yarn that's needed to finish a project.

   Would that take ten days?

   Probably not.

Tea with Eric's kids was stressful.

I'm so glad we're all finally together! I'm so sorry that Melody isn't here yet. She probably lost track of time.

I'm sure she'll be here any minute.

I couldn't tell my mom that Melody was gone right before tea. She's been so excited about getting the families together.

You wussed out. I so wussed out.

But she was still pretty upset.

Mel, call me the minute you get this message. We're all at the restaurant and we're going to have to start without you.

And the dads were suspicious.

Do you know where Melody is?

Nope.

Well, you didn't exactly lie.

After tea Eric went out with his kids and Mom and I went home. When we got there I showed her Melody's note and she **FREAKED OUT.**

Why didn't you tell me this before???

I wanted you to enjoy your tea...

I have to find your sister. But this is NOT OVER.

Then she started calling Melody's friends. I felt completely useless, so I left.

So what do we do now?

Want to wrap a tree?

FACT: Declan is currently driving to Pueblo, Colorado.

FACT: My dad lives in Pueblo.

FACT: Melody doesn't have her driver's license yet.

Or a car.

FACT: Melody and Declan are friends.

CONCLUSION:

Declan is driving Melody to Colorado to see our dad.

Because Melody has unfinished business with him.

We have to tell my mom.

We think we know where Melody is. Or at least where she's going.

When we told them what we'd found out, Lydia's mom became frantic, but Coach Eric calmed her down and started to make arrangements to fly to Colorado to get Melody. The first flight we could book is on Christmas Day.

You know, you could stay with us while they get Melody.

No. My sister needs me. But save me some of Papa Dad's fruitcake.

Really?

No. Please don't.

PAPA DAD's FAMOUS FRUITCAKE

Alternative uses:
Hammer! Paperweight!
Intimidating
Weapon!

For the love of Kami, put the fruitcake down!

Lydia, her mom, and Coach Eric are on a flight to Colorado to get Melody, leaving Daddy and Papa Dad in charge of all the final wedding preparations.

We have a week until the wedding.

Lydia's mom kept all of her planning in a big binder. A lot of the stuff is already taken care of, but a lot of it isn't.

I decided to call Roland to see if he was available to help, but he wasn't there.

Hi, this is Julie, we're at Lydia's working on a big project and I could really use your help — please call me!

It was weird when he didn't call me back. Roland usually calls back in four seconds.

Reasons Why Roland Isn't Calling Back

1. He's trapped under something heavy.

2. He's been abducted by aliens.

3. No one gave him the message. Maybe I should call back?

Getting on a plane to find Melody felt like an adventure, but a really not fun one.

Pack enough for three days, we're not going to be there long.

My mom called my dad to ask if he'd seen Melody and they got into a big fight on the phone.

I didn't **LOSE** her, Gerald, and as usual, yelling at me is **NOT HELPING**

So we guess that she's still on the road.

The plan is to get to Pueblo and then wait for Melody at Dad's house, which does not sound very fun. I can't imagine what my dad and Coach Eric will have to talk about.

goldstandard3000: We're here.

jladybugaboo: Is Melody there yet?

goldstandard3000: No, but we just got here. Brenna is letting me use her computer while Dad and Coach Eric stare at each other.

jladybugaboo: How long have you been there?

goldstandard3000: Three hours. I think we're going to go back to the hotel soon, though, because this is super lame.

jladybugaboo: Is your dad happy to see you?

goldstandard3000: He said, "Oh, good, your hair isn't that awful blue anymore."

When we got to Dad's house today, no one wanted to go in.

Do we have to go in?

Where else are we going to wait?

Here. In the car.

I've got cards.

We played gin rummy until Declan's car finally pulled around the corner with Melody in the passenger seat.

goldstandard3000: We got Melody.

jladybugaboo: YES!!! Is she okay? Did your mom kill her?

goldstandard3000: Yes and no.

jladybugaboo: So what happened?

goldstandard3000: We were waiting in the car when Declan pulled up.

jladybugaboo: Like a police stakeout!

goldstandard3000: Exactly, only Mom got annoyed every time I called her "Sarge."

jladybugaboo: Wow. So you just left?

goldstandard3000: We went back to the hotel. Mel, Mom, and I are in one room, and Declan is staying with Coach Eric in the other one.

Do you want to see your dad tomorrow?

What's the point? He's going to be annoyed that I've messed up his perfect Christmastime with his perfect family and his perfect stupid lawn penguins. I just want to go home.

I'm so sorry, sweetie. Lydia, why don't you go with Eric and Declan to find dinner.

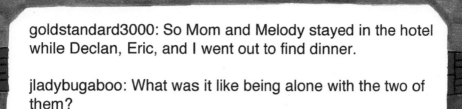

goldstandard3000: So Mom and Melody stayed in the hotel while Declan, Eric, and I went out to find dinner.

jladybugaboo: What was it like being alone with the two of them?

goldstandard3000: Awkward at first.

I'm so glad you're here. I think Eric wants to kill me.

You drove my sister to Colorado. I kind of want to kill you.

Is there any way I can win in this situation?

I get your fortune cookie.

jladybugaboo: Crazy.

goldstandard3000: So now Declan and Eric are going to drive Declan's car back home and Mom is trying to get the next available flight back for the rest of us. How are all the wedding preparations going?

jladybugaboo: Okay. It would be going quicker if Roland were here to help but I've called him four times and he hasn't called back.

goldstandard3000: Is he upset because you didn't show up for Christmas Eve?

jladybugaboo: Oh no.

goldstandard3000: You totally forgot.

jladybugaboo: I totally forgot. Do you think he's mad?

goldstandard3000: You called him four times and he hasn't called back. Unless he's trapped under something heavy or he was kidnapped by aliens, I'd say he's probably mad.

jladybugaboo: What do I do???

goldstandard3000: In my experience, the best thing to do is to apologize.

I have to apologize to Roland for ditching him on Christmas Eve. It's weird — this whole time I haven't really been sure that I even want him to be my boyfriend, and the moment he stops acting like my boyfriend I feel awful. And I still don't know if I want him to be my boyfriend but I definitely hate that he's mad and not talking to me.

Then Roland and I had The Talk.

Sometimes I wonder if you even want to date.

I do! Kind of. I liked skating.

Really? You fell twelve times.

But it was fun. Way more fun than hanging out with Chuck and Jane.

I thought you wanted to hang out with them.

But I thought you wanted to hang out with them.

It's amazing how much not talking about stuff can lead to confusion and badness.

And then he kissed me. It was nice.

Eric and Declan left today to drive Declan's car back home.

Okay, stop shaking. We have a long drive ahead of us and I can't have you terrified of me the entire time.

Okay, Mr. Wexler.

But I'm in charge of the radio.

Whatever you say, Mr. Wexler.

Our flight back home leaves tomorrow, so we spent the entire day in the hotel room eating pizza and watching movies in our pajamas.

Best bachelorette party ever!

I hope the wedding prep is going okay.

I thought that the wedding prep was going okay until...

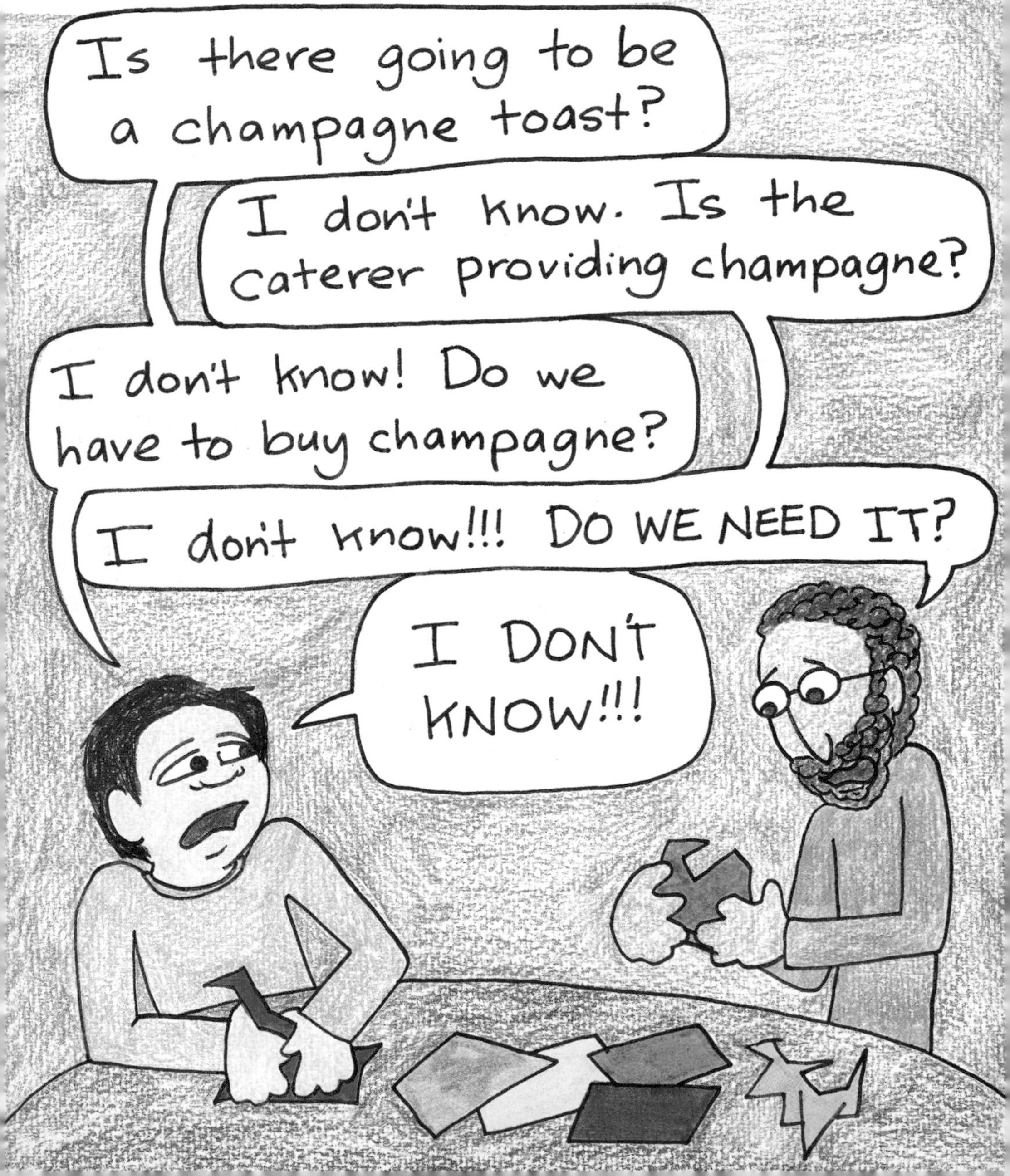

I'm used to one of my parents freaking out while the other one stays calm, like how Papa Dad helps Daddy to not pass out when we're on a plane, or how Daddy has kept Papa Dad from getting too hysterical about Roland. I have never seen them both losing it at the same time.

ARE WE SERIOUSLY SUPPOSED TO FOLD 1,000 PAPER CRANES?

WE'LL NEVER BE ABLE TO FINISH ON TIME AND THEN WE'LL HAVE FAILED ELAINE!

SHE DESERVES BETTER THAN THIS!!!

GAAAHHH!!!

It was terrifying. I had to do something.

What's he doing here?
DADS. Calm down. David and Lori are going to talk to the caterer. Ellie is in charge of flowers and decorating the house for the wedding. Roland is going to write out all the tablecards because he has nice handwriting, and I don't know why Jamie is here but I guess he's helping, too.
He's actually very good at origami.
Really?
Great! Let's get to work.

goldstandard3000: You bossed everyone around?

jladybugaboo: I totally did!!!

goldstandard3000: How on earth did that happen?!?

jladybugaboo: I just thought to myself, What would Lydia do? And then suddenly I was telling everyone what to do.

goldstandard3000: I don't always tell everyone what to do.

jladybugaboo: And then when I was done I was a little dizzy.

goldstandard3000: Being bossy is a lot of work.

jladybugaboo: I felt all confident when everyone just got to work, and it seemed like a good time to talk to Papa Dad.

Roland is here because he wants to help. He's a great guy and you should be nicer to him.
I don't know what you're talking about...
Papa Dad, you've been acting crazy ever since we started hanging out.
Hanging out? I thought you and Roland were Dating.
It doesn't matter what you call it, he's my friend and we like being together. You've been weird and rude to him and it's disrespectful, especially when he's always been super nice to you. And to me.
You're right.

Then we talked for a little while about how it's hard for him to see me growing up and how if Roland ever breaks my heart Papa Dad is going to break both of his legs. The more we talked, the less stressed-out we felt, and making paper cranes got a lot easier. It helped that Jamie really knew what he was doing.

You want to try to make the folds as precise as possible in the beginning, because it makes things a lot easier in the end.

Please don't break my legs.

Once everyone really calmed down and got to work, everything began to run smoothly.
The napkins should be ecru, not off-white. Ecru!
Your dads are really into this.
Well, they never got to have a wedding for themselves. When I get married, they're going to lose their minds. If I get married. In fifty years. Maybe.
So there's hope.

And Papa Dad actually started being nice to Roland.

It was a relief to see Papa Dad acting like himself again. I know he's still weirded out about Roland, but he's trying really hard to be normal (or normal for him, anyway) and that's good enough. Actually, it's great.

After a full day of vegging out we all seemed to feel better, and the trip home was mostly uneventful.

The flight attendant thinks I'm crazy.

Since when do you care what people think?

You know what? I don't.

I think Melody is going to be okay. Like Mom told us, sometimes people just need to know they're loved.

Coming home was amazing.

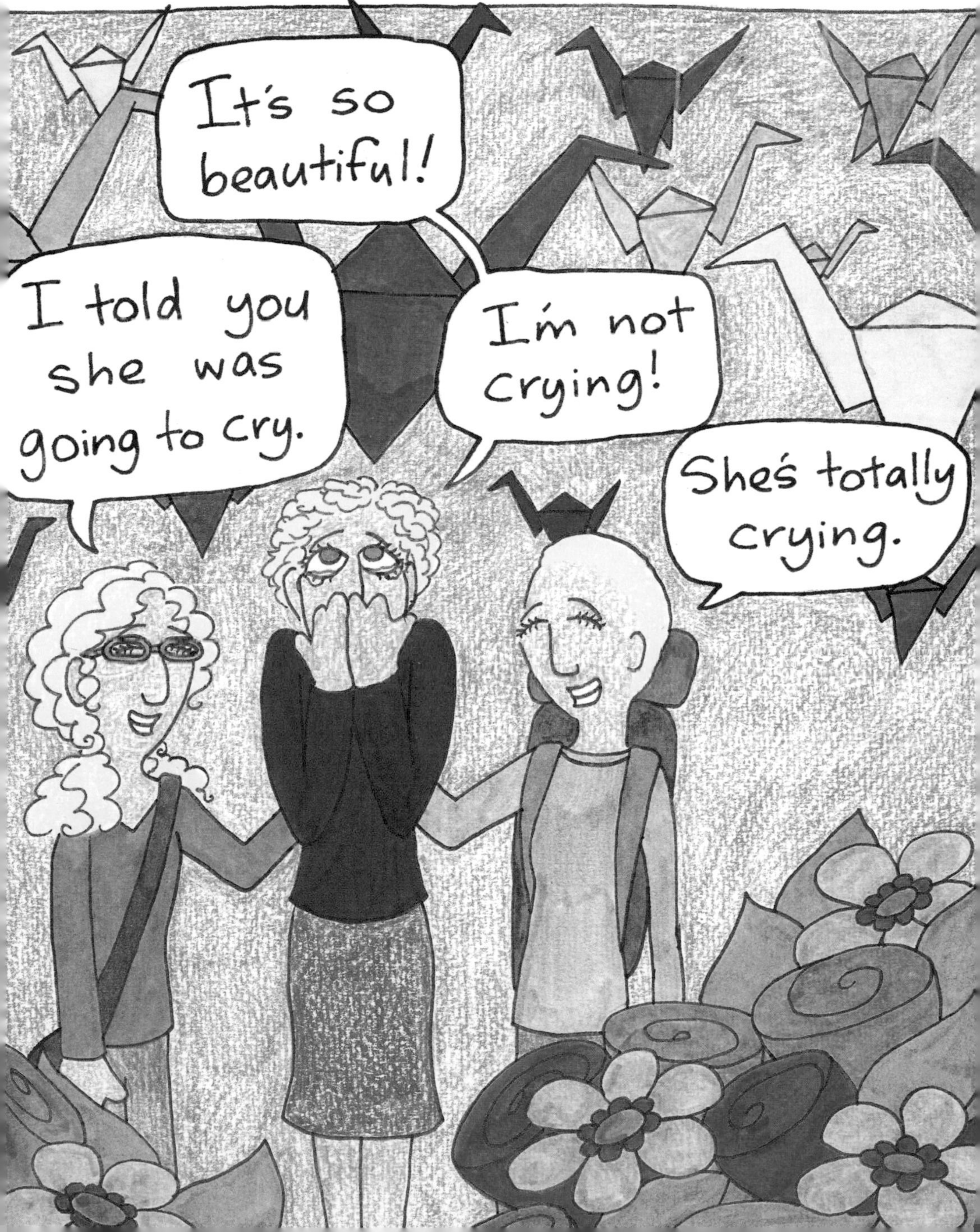

jladybugaboo: So, are you ready for tomorrow?

goldstandard3000: I think so. I can't believe that my mom invited Jamie.

jladybugaboo: He folded 946 paper cranes. I think he earned it.

goldstandard3000: True. But now I'm stuck with him for the entire wedding.

jladybugaboo: He's actually not that bad. He's kind of funny.

goldstandard3000: He once tried to ride a dog.

jladybugaboo: It was a pretty big dog.

goldstandard3000: But it wasn't, you know, A HORSE.

Last night Eric sat down with Melody and me and we had a talk.

I know I'm not your father, but I think I'm very lucky that I get to be your stepfather, and I want you to know that I'm here for you and your mum.

Then he gave us Claddagh rings from Ireland.

Melody and I agreed that they're kind of cheesy.

Loyalty

Friendship

Love

But you're both wearing them.

Yeah, we are.

The wedding was great, and the first dance was... lovely.

There are places I remember...
doo dee doooooo dee, la la lala
I didn't have much time
to rehearse for this,
In my life in my life lala...

Was it really that bad?
No one tried to attack you or smash your guitar, so that's progress.
Yay me!

The reception was fun. It was really great to see everyone relaxed and having a good time—even Melody.

I thought Melody and Declan were grounded for life.

They are, but Eric begged Declan's parents to let him come to the wedding. Being in a car together for three days straight made them besties.

And you had a good time dancing with Jamie.
I did not!
Not even a little?
You only like me because Jen told you I wanted a boyfriend.
That's not true. I like you because you're brave and funny and pretty and I think it's amazing what you do to keep the trees warm.
So you like me because I knit for trees? That's crazy.
So is wrapping a tree in yarn.
Okay, a little.

Acknowledgments

I would like to send a universe full of gratitude to the wonderful team at Amulet Books: Susan Van Metre, James Armstrong, Jen Graham, Melissa Arnst, Chris Blank, Chad Beckerman, Robyn Ng, Laura Mihalick, Morgan Dubin, and the tremendous Jason Wells. Overflowing buckets of love and thanks are due to Maggie Lehrman, my dear editor who understands that MORE UNICORNS can fix nearly any storyline snafu.

Thanks as always to the amazing Dan Lazar, who has been graciously putting up with my Hey, It's 4 a.m., What Do You Think About This Wacky Idea? e-mails for the past eight years, as well as Torie Doherty-Munro and all the supportive people at Writers House.

And last but never least, thanks to my favorite date ever, Mark, and our daughter, Anya, whose championship-level napping skills made it possible to get this book in on deadline.

About the Author

Amy Ignatow is the author and illustrator of The Popularity Papers series. She is a graduate of Moore College of Art and Design and can fold many origami cranes. Amy lives in Philadelphia with her husband, Mark, their daughter, Anya, and their cat, Mathilda, who is an unrepentant gnawer of colored pencils.